Come On, Dad!

Written by Louise John
Illustrated by Catalina Alvarez

WAYLAND

"This is a steep hill," said Cara.

"Yes," said Mum. "Let's go up to the top."

"This is fun," said Olly.

"Yes," said Cara.
"Let's get to the top!
Keep going!"

9

"I am hot. Let's stop.
I want a rest!" said Dad.

"No rest," said Mum.
"We want to get to
the top. Come on, Dad!"

"This is no fun!" said
Dad. "This hill is too
steep. I want a rest."

14

"Come on, Dad!" said Olly. "We want to get to the top."

"Look!" said Mum.
"We are at the top
of the hill!"

"Oh no!" said Cara.
"Where is Dad?"

Guiding a First Read of
Come On, Dad!

It is important to talk through the book with the child before they read it alone. This prepares them for the way the story unfolds, and allows them to enjoy the pictures as you both talk naturally, using the language they will later encounter when reading. Read them the brief overview, and then follow the suggestions below:

1. Talking through the book
The family were walking up a very steep hill. Mum, Olly and Cara all wanted to get to the top, but Dad was hot and he wanted a rest. "Come on, Dad!" they told him, but when they got to the top, where was Dad?

Let's read the title: **Come On, Dad!**
On page 4, Cara is looking up at the hill. This is a steep hill, isn't it?
Turn over to page 6. Mum said, "Let's go up to the top."
And on page 8, Olly and Cara think it's fun, "Keep going!"

Continue through the book, guiding the discussion to fit the text as the child looks at the illustrations.

On page 18, Mum and the children were happy as they were at the top of the hill. Turn over. Oh no! "Where's Dad?" said Cara. Where do you think he was?

2. A first reading of the book

Ask the child to read the book independently, pointing carefully underneath each word (tracking), while thinking about the story. Praise attempts by the child to correct themselves, and prompt them to use their letter knowledge, the punctuation, and check the meaning, for example:

You said, "This is a step hill." Does that make sense? Try that again. Good, you stopped at 'steep'. See those two 'ee's'? Now say the word with 'e-e' in the middle.

I like the way you make Olly and Cara sound excited.

3. Follow-up activities

The high frequency words in this title are:

a   get   is   no   said   the   this   to   want   we

- Select two high frequency words, and ask the child to find them throughout the book. Discuss the shape of the letters and their letter sounds.
- To memorise the words, ask the child to write them in the air, then write them repeatedly on a whiteboard or on paper, leaving a space between each attempt.

4. Encourage

- Reading the book again – with expression.
- Drawing a picture based on the story.
- Writing one or two sentences using the practised words.

START READING is a series of highly enjoyable books for beginner readers. **The books have been carefully graded to match the Book Bands widely used in schools.** This enables readers to be sure they choose books that match their own reading ability.

Look out for the Band colour on the book in our Start Reading logo.

The Bands are:

Pink Band 1A & 1B

Red Band 2

Yellow Band 3

Blue Band 4

Green Band 5

Orange Band 6

Turquoise Band 7

Purple Band 8

Gold Band 9

START READING books can be read independently or shared with an adult. They promote the enjoyment of reading through satisfying stories supported by fun illustrations.

Louise John is really the editor of Start Reading, but wanted to see how she liked writing books, too. It was quite tricky, but she found that eating lots of chocolate biscuits made her think better! She tries out her ideas on her daughter, Amelia, who tells her if they are any good or not!

Catalina Alvarez lives in Sherwood, Nottingham with her son Oscar and two cats called Lizzie and Winnie. She has illustrated more books than she can count, especially lots of phonics books. Her favourite one is called 'Pog the Dog!'